This book belongs to:

Jordan

1. HUCKLE'S HOUSE
2. HILDA'S HOUSE
3. SGT. MURPHY'S
4. PIG FAMILY HOUSE
5. MR FRUMBLE'S
6. FIRE STATION
7. TOWN HALL
8. MR FIXIT'S HOUSE
9. BUSYTOWN HOSPITAL
10. SCHOOLHOUSE
11. MR GRONKLE'S
12. SPROUT'S FARM

THE RECYCLING PLANT

BUSYTOWN AIRPORT

STADIUM

APRIL RHINO'S HOUSE

THE PORT

MOUNT BUSY
OBSERVATORY

SKI CHALET

Welcome to Busytown!

CAMPING GROUNDS

BUSY BAY
POINT

BRUNO'S
SNACK
STAND

THE BEACH

THE
TRAIN
STATION

BUSYTOWN GRAND HOTEL

SEA FORT

First published in Great Britain in 1994
by HarperCollins Publishers Ltd,
77-85 Fulham Palace Road,
Hammersmith, London W6 8JB
10 9 8 7 6 5 4 3 2 1
Copyright © 1994 the Estate of Richard Scarry
Adapted from the animated television series
The Busy World of Richard Scarry (TM)
produced by Paramount Pictures and Cinar
All rights reserved.
ISBN: 0 00 664549 6
Printed and bound in Italy
Designed and produced by Les Livres du Dragon d'Or.

The Busy World of Richard Scarry

Mr Frumble's New Cars

Collins

An Imprint of HarperCollinsPublishers

Mr Frumble drives his pickle car through Busytown. Suddenly, a gust of wind blows his hat off. "Oh dear!" says Mr Frumble, looking behind him. His hat is hooked on the tail of his car. He reaches out for it. "Ooops! Ahhh!"

Oh no! Look out, Mr Frumble!
HONK! HONK!
Crassshhh!

"Don't worry, Mr Frumble,"
Mr Fixit assures him.
"I'll fix your car so that
it's better than new."

Sergeant Murphy
arrives at the
scene. "I'm sorry
Mr Frumble, but
I have to give
you a ticket.
It's the law."
"Oh dear,"
mutters Mr Frumble.

UMFF!

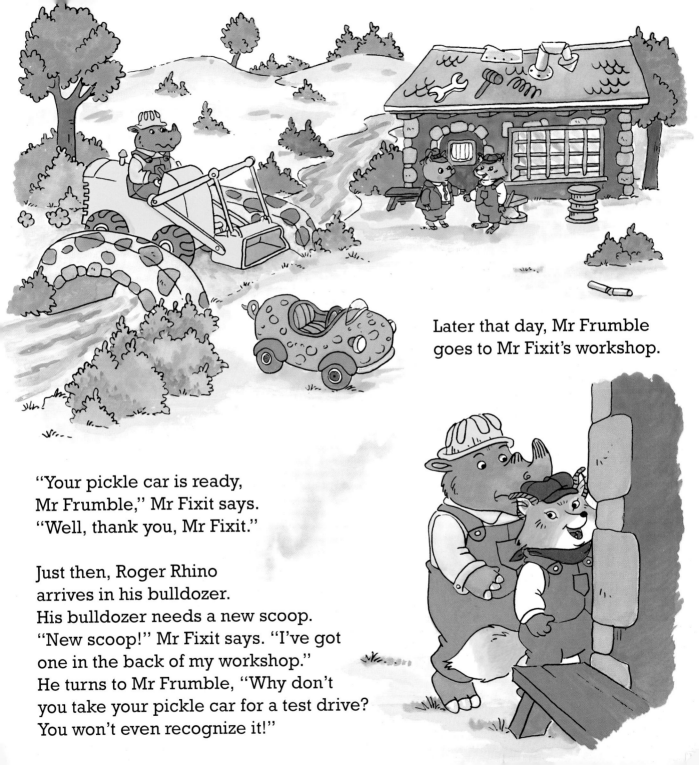

Later that day, Mr Frumble goes to Mr Fixit's workshop.

"Your pickle car is ready, Mr Frumble," Mr Fixit says. "Well, thank you, Mr Fixit."

Just then, Roger Rhino arrives in his bulldozer. His bulldozer needs a new scoop. "New scoop!" Mr Fixit says. "I've got one in the back of my workshop." He turns to Mr Frumble, "Why don't you take your pickle car for a test drive? You won't even recognize it!"

Mr Frumble walks over to the pickle car.
"But I recognize this car!" exclaims Mr Frumble.

"It can't be mine – Mr Fixit told me I wouldn't recognize it!"
Then Mr Frumble sees the bulldozer.
He climbs on the seat, starts it up and drives away.

"My goodness!" he says. "I certainly don't recognise this one."

Nearby, Sergeant Murphy is helping people to cross the busy street.

VROOM!
Watch out Sergeant Murphy!

He jumps out of the way just in time. That was a close call!

"Help! Help, Sergeant Murphy!" shouts Roger Rhino.
"Mr Frumble has taken my bulldozer!"
"He can't drive the bulldozer any better than he can drive his pickle car!" Sergeant Murphy says. "I'll have to give him another ticket!"

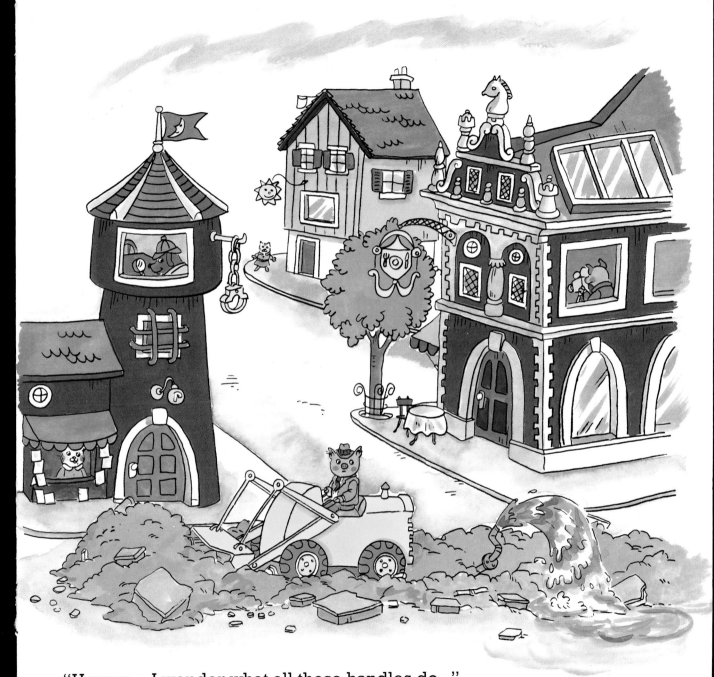

"Hmmm... I wonder what all these handles do..."
Mr Frumble pulls and shoves. Clonk! Watch out! Mr Frumble puts the
scoop down. **OOOOOPS! CRASH!** The scoop has dug up the street!

Soon a big crowd gathers on the square.
"What's happened?"
"Who dug this big hole?"
"Are they building a new town hall?"
people wonder.

"What is everyone looking at?" thinks
Mr Frumble, walking towards a car
nearby.

He climbs inside and closes the door. Hilda hasn't noticed that her taxi has a new driver!

Mayor Fox calls Sergeant Murphy from his office. "Get down here fast! Mr Frumble just bulldozed the town square and has taken off in a taxi!"

"Oh no, now I have a taxi to catch!" Sergeant Murphy says and speeds away, his siren blaring.

Mr Frumble looks at the taxi metre.

"What a noisy clock Mr Fixit has installed. I better go back and get it fixed."

"But I need to go to the airport!" Hilda shouts.
"Hilda Hippo!" Mr Frumble exclaims. "What a surprise."
"Mr Frumble?" she says, puzzled, "I have to meet my cousin in ten minutes!"

"Well in that case, we had better step on it!" Mr Frumble makes a U-turn and speeds away in the opposite direction.

CRASSHH! The car leaves the road.
Mr Frumble drives through the fence to the aeroplane
and right up the loading ramp.

"AHHHHHHH!"
Hilda screams,
running away.

"I wonder where Hilda went?" Mr Frumble mutters.
Meanwhile, Rudolf von Flugel lands his aeroplane.
"Why is everyone in such a hurry?" Mr Frumble wonders
and climbs into the driver's seat.

Up, up
and away
he flies!

"Mr von Flugel, have you seen
Mr Frumble?" Sergeant Murphy
asks, arriving on his motorcycle.

"He just took off in my plane!"
Rudolf answers.

Rudolf's plane zooms through
the sky, zig-zagging, diving
and looping-the-loop.
"My, what a smooth ride!"
Mr Frumble exclaims.
Turning over, he loses his hat.
Oh no, not again Mr Frumble!
The plane dives through the sky.

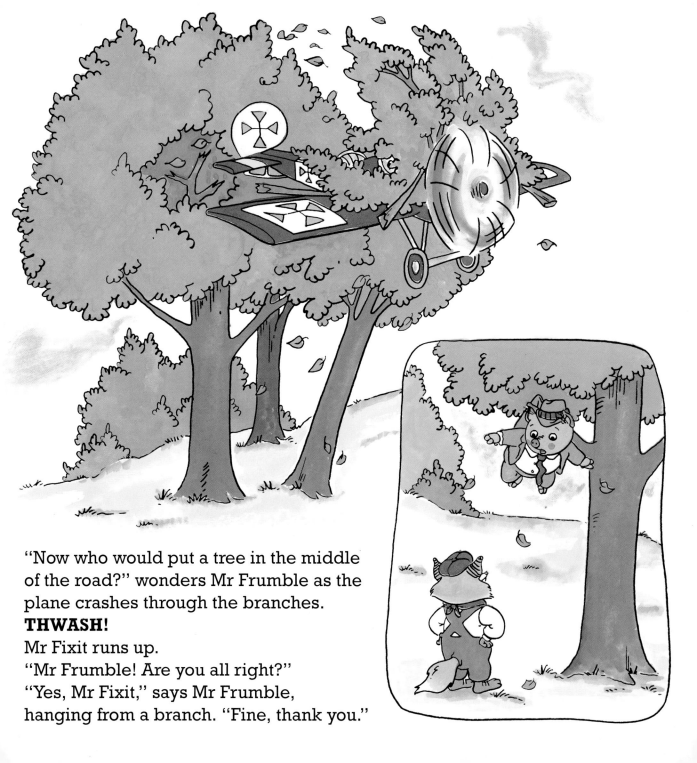

"Now who would put a tree in the middle of the road?" wonders Mr Frumble as the plane crashes through the branches.
THWASH!
Mr Fixit runs up.
"Mr Frumble! Are you all right?"
"Yes, Mr Fixit," says Mr Frumble, hanging from a branch. "Fine, thank you."

BUMP! THUMP! Down comes Mr Frumble! And down comes his hat.

"Mr Fixit," says Mr Frumble, getting up, "Do you remember you told me I wouldn't recognize my car? Well, I wonder if you could fix my car so I COULD recognize it?"

"I tried to tell you before," answers Mr Fixit, pointing. "Your pickle car has been here all the time!"

SCREECH!
Sergeant Murphy pulls up on his motorcycle. "Now that I've caught up with you Mr Frumble," he says, "I have a few tickets to give you!"
Sergeant Murphy pulls out his ticket book:

"This one's for failure to stop for an officer... This one's for digging a hole without a permit... This one's for illegal tree trimming..."

... and this one's for littering."
Poor Mr Frumble!
"Dear me, I think I will go now," Mr Frumble sighs.
He climbs into the driver's seat one more time.

"Wait! Mr Frumble!" Sergeant Murphy shouts.

"That's MY motorcycle!"

1. HUCKLE'S HOUSE
2. HILDA'S HOUSE
3. SGT. MURPHY'S
4. PIG FAMILY HOUSE
5. MR FRUMBLE'S
6. FIRE STATION
7. TOWN HALL
8. MR FIXIT'S HOUSE
9. BUSYTOWN HOSPITAL
10. SCHOOLHOUSE
11. MR GRONKLE'S
12. SPROUT'S FARM

THE RECYCLING PLANT

BUSYTOWN AIRPORT

THE FLOUR MILL

STADIUM

APRIL RHINO'S HOUSE

THE PORT

MOUNT BUSY
OBSERVATORY

Welcome to
Busytown!

SKI CHALET

CAMPING GROUNDS

BUSY BAY
POINT

BRUNO'S
SNACK
STAND

THE BEACH

THE
TRAIN
STATION

BUSYTOWN GRAND HOTEL

SEA FORT